"Just play. Have fun. Enjoy the game."

– Michael Jordan

First Edition
Kane Miller, A Division of EDC Publishing

Text and illustrations copyright © Richard Torrey 2014

Kane Miller, A Division of EDC Publishing
PO Box 470663
Tulsa, OK 74147-0663
www.kanemiller.com
www.edcpub.com
www.usbornebooksandmore.com

Library of Congress Control Number: 2013953404

Manufactured by Regent Publishing Services, Hong Kong
Printed March 2014 in ShenZhen, Guangdong, China

ISBN: 978-1-61067-286-3

1 2 3 4 5 6 7 8 9 10

A BASKETBALL Story

By Richard Torrey

Kane Miller
A DIVISION OF EDC PUBLISHING

Every day after school, I practice basketball with my big brother, Alan.

First we warm up by bouncing the ball without looking at it. That's called dribbling.

Then we take turns making baskets.
That's called a shootaround.

When Alan and his friends play games, they sometimes let me play too!

Alan is lucky because he also plays on a *real* basketball team, in a *real* basketball league, with *real* basketball jerseys!
You have to be twelve to play on that team.
I'm not even eight.

But today I'm the lucky one because today *I* get to play on a *real* basketball team, in a *real* basketball league. We even get *real* basketball jerseys!

My team is the Wildcats. That's the same team Alan played on when he was my age.

I even have the same coach – Mr. Clarke.
Alan says Mr. Clarke is the best coach ever!

Mr. Clarke tells us to call him Coach Jon. He says we're going to work hard and have fun at the same time.

He also tells us we have to practice "the basics." I think that means we have to practice *everything*.

And we do.

We practice dribbling without looking at the ball,
just like my big brother, Alan, taught me.

And when Coach Jon blows his whistle we practice dribbling and running at the same time. We run all around the floor, which is called the *basketball court*.

We practice passing, just like Alan taught me.
There are two kinds of passes.

Good pass,
Number Eight.

Bounce!

Thanks.
You too.

Bounce!

One kind of pass you bounce on purpose.

And one kind of pass you try not to bounce.

Then comes the best thing – *shooting!*

Coach Jon says the secret is to look at the top of the basket when we shoot.

We do free throws – the hardest ...

While we all get a drink of water, Coach Jon tells us he has a surprise.

We're going to a play a practice game against another *real* basketball team!

Even though it's my first game against a *real* basketball team, I'm not even nervous.

That's because it feels just like when I play with my big brother, Alan, and his friends.

In the game, we do all of the things we just practiced.

We dribble.

We pass.

And we shoot!

When it's over, I can't wait to play the next game!

I really am lucky because now I'm on a *real* basketball team, in a *real* basketball league, with the best coach ever!

But mostly I'm lucky because I have the best big brother ever!

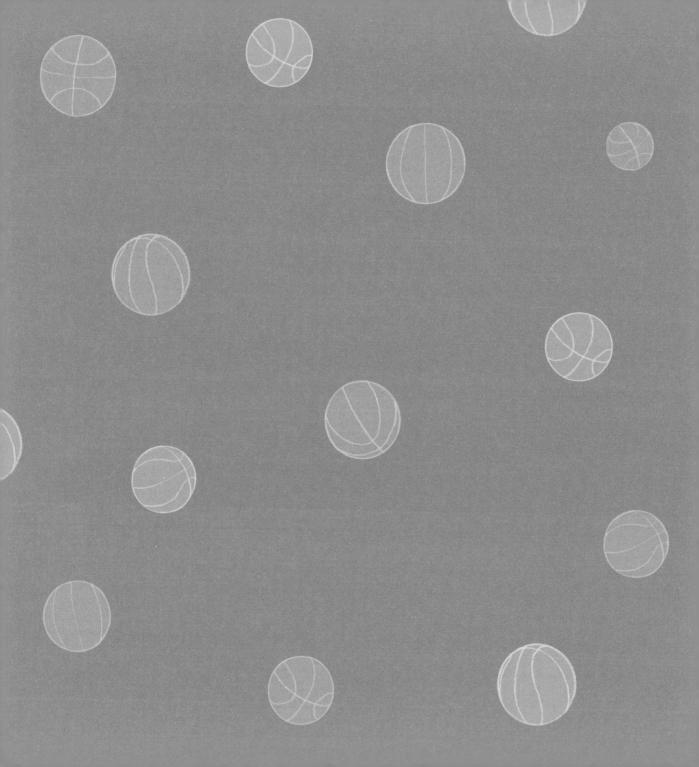